The Young Artist

The Young Artist

THOMAS LOCKER

Dial Books NEW YORK

LATE ONE SPRING AFTERNOON I was putting the final brush strokes on an important portrait when I was suddenly interrupted by heavy pounding on the door. Wilhelm Van der Weld, who runs the watermill near the royal castle, came into my studio to ask my advice. Handing me a stack of drawings, he said, "I don't know what to do about my son, Adrian. All he ever wants to do is draw and dream about becoming an artist. Will you look at his pictures and tell me if he has any talent?"

I had given up teaching some years ago, but reluctantly I agreed to look at the boy's drawings. They were amazing! Immediately I offered to become the gifted lad's teacher. So a few days after his twelfth birthday Adrian said good-bye to his parents and came to my studio to learn the artist's craft.

In my time I've taught a lot of apprentices but never one like Adrian. I remember his first day in the studio. When I gave him a sheet of paper and some black chalk and told him to copy a plaster statue, Adrian looked up at me and said, "I already know how to draw! I want to learn how to use oil paints. I want to make big paintings of the trees, the clouds, and the royal castle!"

"All in good time," I replied. "But first let's see how well you can draw the statue." A few minutes later he proudly showed me his drawing. It was very good but the head was too large and the legs were short. I corrected it and said, "Erase it and draw it again and again until it is exactly right."

Adrian became a good apprentice. Cheerfully he washed my brushes, mixed the paint, and swept the studio. He worked very hard at learning to draw accurately, and after just one year I began to teach him how to paint. He became very good at painting pictures of people. He did a portrait of me that was so well done that I had it framed and even hung it next to some of my own paintings. A good portrait painter is always in demand, so I tried to encourage him. But painting portraits wasn't what Adrian Van der Weld longed to do.

He said that it made him nervous to paint pictures of strangers, especially when they criticized his work before it was finished. Whenever the young fellow had a spare moment, he would wander out into the countryside near his father's mill and draw some trees and the castle. He longed to capture the sparkle of the changing light and the feeling of the wind in the trees. However, it's very difficult for an artist to survive painting only landscapes, so I worried about Adrian's future. Then one day the top chef at the palace, who occasionally bought some of my paintings, came to the studio. He was very impressed by Adrian's portrait of me and asked if the lad could paint his picture. At first I thought that it would be a good idea, but I know now that I made a terrible mistake when I insisted that Adrian paint that portrait.

When Adrian finished the portrait, it looked exactly like the chef. I doubt if I could have done much better myself. But the chef wasn't as pleased and he asked Adrian to change it to make him look younger. He kept saying that there was a little something wrong about the mouth. Adrian was very upset. Later, when I suggested that the chef might not pay unless he was satisfied, Adrian said furiously, "You have always taught me to paint the truth, and now you want me to paint a lie? I can't! I won't!"

Adrian vowed then never to paint another portrait as long as he lived.

Adrian refused to rework the chef's portrait. But when the man returned, he was in a better mood and he looked at the picture again and didn't even realize that Adrian hadn't made the changes he requested. "It's a masterpiece!" he exclaimed.

I wouldn't let Adrian say a word. The honest lad still had a lot to learn about surviving as an artist, but now there were things he'd have to learn on his own. So I gave him the chef's entire payment and suggested that he use it to set up his own studio.

Adrian did, and he started right in painting the castle. However, he soon discovered, when he couldn't sell a single painting, that the king was feared throughout the land and no one wanted a picture of his castle. But just about the time that Adrian's money was almost gone, the royal baker and the king's tailor asked Adrian to paint their portraits.

Adrian then had to make a choice between giving up being an artist altogether or making a compromise. He chose to do the portraits. However, he continued to paint landscapes in his spare time. His work kept improving and he was pleased with his progress. To thank the chef for his help Adrian gave him one of his best pictures of the castle.

Then one day a messenger from the palace arrived with an order bearing the royal seal. It commanded Adrian to appear at the court. At first Adrian was excited, thinking that the chef must have shown the king his picture of the castle. On the way he stopped at the mill to share the wonderful news with his parents. But as he approached the castle, he began to worry. Why had the king ordered him to bring along his paints and brushes? A fierce-looking soldier unlocked the heavy iron gates. For the first time in his life Adrian entered the castle and the gates clanged shut behind him.

Another guard ushered Adrian into the throne room, which was filled with proud ladies and gentlemen dressed in such finery that Adrian felt ashamed of his own humble clothes. Except for the king's only child, the beloved little Princess Helena, who smiled at Adrian, everyone else seemed to look down on him contemptuously.

The king addressed Adrian: "We have decided that you will paint a large picture that will include portraits of all twenty-seven members of my court."

Adrian gasped and protested, "But Your Highness, I am really a landscape painter. I've never attempted a group portrait. It would take years to complete, and besides, I can only finish a painting in private, and—"

But the king interrupted him, saying that he could take as much time as he needed, and ordered that Adrian wasn't to be disturbed. Dismissing him the king told a servant to show Adrian to a room in the tower. To his dismay Adrian saw that it contained a table, a chair, a bed, and an easel holding a huge, blank canvas.

It was like a bad dream, but the next day was a nightmare. Adrian found himself cornered by the courtiers.

"Take off my fat," warned the minister of finance, "or you will spend the rest of your life in the dungeon."

"Paint me standing up straight," hissed the old duchess, "or I will see to it that you are hanged from the gallows!"

Every one of the noblemen and noblewomen, except for the little princess, threatened Adrian and demanded that he improve their appearance in the court portrait. My poor apprentice, who only wanted to paint people as he truly saw them, felt trapped. So using the excuse that he would need more paint for such a large painting, he fled from the castle to ask my advice.

At first I was very glad to see Adrian, but when I learned about his dangerous situation, I blamed myself for having insisted that he paint the chef's portrait. I had to come up with a plan to help the boy through this ordeal. I knew that he could make accurate drawings of the nobles with ease, but that he couldn't paint with them looking over his shoulder. So I suggested that he make drawings of everyone in the throne room until they were all satisfied with their likenesses, and then Adrian should retreat to the tower and combine the drawings into a large composition in the privacy and safety of the studio. As he left, I said, "It is a great honor to be asked to do a court portrait." Adrian shook his head and replied, "To paint twenty-six lies is no honor." Slowly he returned to the castle to begin the most difficult time of his life. I honestly thought I might never see him again.

Six months passed as Adrian worked in the throne room. All the while he was bullied and badgered by the vain nobles until at last they were all pleased with the drawings. Finally Adrian took the studies to the tower to begin painting. But, except for the picture of the young princess, which was inspired, Adrian's work was false and lifeless. Everyone seemed the same. The men all looked handsome and the women were beautiful. The next morning he laid out his paints, but he couldn't bring himself to pick up a brush. All that day he sat and stared at the huge, empty canvas until the light in the studio began to fade. Then the tired and frightened lad decided to take a walk on the palace grounds to look at the trees and clouds that he longed to paint.

A cool evening breeze moved through the trees as he approached the royal arch. There Adrian met the little princess. Her smile seemed especially beautiful in the evening light and Adrian made a quick sketch of her. The next day, because he hadn't painted at all for six months, he decided to warm up for the court portrait by painting a small picture of the princess. It turned out well and gave him the confidence to begin work on the huge canvas. But he couldn't forget the threats of the nobles and the work progressed slowly. Sometimes he was so afraid he wouldn't be able to please them that he couldn't paint at all. In these dark moods he would ask the Princess Helena to pose, and that always seemed to help him.

Months turned into a year and then two years passed. The noblemen and noblewomen had grown impatient to see their portraits. In spite of the king's order not to disturb Adrian, a group of the courtiers banded together and climbed the stairs to the studio. Princess Helena saw them and ran to warn the king.

When they entered the studio, the noble ladies and gentlemen were outraged to find the room filled with paintings of the princess, but the court portrait barely started. Then the king, furious that his order had been disobeyed, rushed up the stairs and stormed in. Immediately his eyes were drawn to one picture after another of his beloved daughter.

"Throw Van der Weld in the dungeon," shouted the minister of finance.

"Hang him," hissed the duchess.

"He must be punished," shrieked the queen.

"On the contrary," the king replied icily. "The artist has painted truly beautiful pictures and we shall reward him."

To punish the nobles for their disobedience, the king told Adrian to paint them exactly the way he saw them. And in no time at all Adrian finished the group portrait. The band of nobles were furious, but the king was so delighted with Adrian's work that he rewarded him with a gift of land and a fine house near his family's mill.

The other day I met my former student out in the countryside. He was teaching his own apprentice how to paint the trees and the clouds, with the towers of the castle far, far in the distance.

To Josette Frank
T. L.

Published by Dial Books
A Division of Penguin Books USA Inc.
2 Park Avenue, New York, New York 10016

Published simultaneously in Canada
by Fitzhenry & Whiteside Limited, Toronto
Copyright © 1989 by Thomas Locker
All rights reserved
Design by Nancy R. Leo
Printed in the U.S.A.
W
First Edition
1 3 5 7 9 10 8 6 4 2

Library of Congress Cataloging in Publication Data

Locker, Thomas, 1937-
The young artist.

Summary: A talented young artist commanded to paint
the king's courtiers, all of whom wish to be portrayed
with improved appearances, struggles with his sense of integrity,
which demands honest portraiture.
[1. Artists—Fiction. 2. Painting—Fiction.
3. Ethics—Fiction.] I. Title.
PZ7,L7945Yo   1989   [Fic]   88-33516
ISBN 0-8037-0625-1
ISBN 0-8037-0627-8 (lib. bdg.)

The art for each picture was created with oil paints.
It was then color-separated and reproduced in full color.